EMBRACE

Recommended for Mature Audiences

Also by
SHIRLEY HOWARD HALL

"LISTEN"

"ONE DAY:
Life, Love and Controversy
in Middle America"

Contributor to:

STARS IN OUR HEARTS: MOMENTS
Edited by Susan Hilary

"CANDY"
Edited by Dale Winslow and Erin Badough

EMBRACE

A Collection of Poems

by
SHIRLEY HOWARD HALL

TULSA OKLAHOMA

EMBRACE is an original publication of
TOTAL PUBLISHING AND MEDIA.

This collection has never before appeared in book form.

Requests for permission to make copies of any part of this work
should be mailed to:

TOTAL PUBLISHING AND MEDIA
5332 South Memorial Drive
Suite 200
Tulsa, OK 74145

www.totalpublishingandmedia.com

Printed in the United States of America.

FIRST EDITION

Recommended for Mature Audiences

All photography by the author

To

Eros

The Greek god of love and sexual desire.

Venus

The Roman goddess of love,
beauty, sex, and sexual seduction

Priapus

The fertility god - protector of male genitalia.

"......Although I may try to
write about love,
I am rendered helpless.
my pen breaks,
and the paper slips away
at the ineffable place
where lover loving and
loved are one......"

Rumi

Foreword

By Art Noble, BSEng.S, MBA

Most men make plaintive cries to *Eros* in the name of their beloved, seeking only what they have learned: control and pleasure. It is by these two devices we, both genders, are deceived. It appears the lust of women ranges far beyond the paraventricular nucleus of the hypothalamus: it permeates the soul! And men must love in order to benefit from it. This is the giving of love through the body in its most intimate and powerful form.

Knowing, and having felt, this ecstasy she is cursed by submitting to the demon of control. She is blessed by the words flowing from her hand and cursed with ecstatic experiences difficult to communicate—but she does. Passion is felt in every line of this book.

As seen in the author's poem *Incubus*, the rape fantasy is the most common sexual fantasy held by women. This fantasy has nothing to do with the horror of its reality. It is only a mechanism to repress the repression imposed upon women in various cultures over the past 5000 years or so. Most modern women are lulled into a sexual sleep. Women, wake up!

And when you do, most modern men won't be able to handle it. The impact of the *Malleus Maleficarum* still dwells within us.

Art Noble, BSEng.S, MBA
Author of *The Sacred Female ~*
A Sonata of Sexual Love and Spirituality.
Published in the US and UK - Read on NPR.
Website/ blogs www.thesacredfemale.com.

Table of Contents

Amour

Adultére

Me faire l'amour

Amour brisé

Tu me manques

Summary

Introduction

When asked to take on this project I questioned why me? I am an advocate for peace, freedom, justice and equality. I write about poverty, unemployment, global warming, religion, war and politics. Who am I to lucidly embrace the subjects of intimacy, sexuality, fulfillment and relationships?

"... you write about real people living real lives.." Hearing these words from a close friend and respected colleague I recognized the parallels. Real people are sexual beings and sex lives range from short-lived gratifications to lifetime journeys - from ecstatic sexual fulfillment to society's cruelest and ugliest atrocities.

I knew inspired by mankind's daytime wishes, nighttime dreams, array of fantasies, non-confronted truths and life long lies I could confrontationally EMBRACE the compassions and complexities of human sexuality. Telling society's multifaceted story in first person I could bring this collection to life.

EMBRACE introduces themes that will heat you up in the most wonderful places, and others that will angrily cool you down. With words you might not recognize and languages you might not understand, you'll connect with an exhumed passion, a flow of emotions, a raging anger, and just maybe an erotic pleasure.

Lines separating love, romance, intimacy, erotica and porn formulate differently in each of us. Predisposed by childhood and adolescence teachings, ethics, education, beliefs, practices, and religious dogmas these lines are ingrained into our psyche;

"what's right is right and what's wrong is wrong."
As adults we learn these lines can and at times should be crossed. We learn the width and depth of each line is negligible and those precious intervals are not set in gold.

"What's good for you might not be good for me or to me; what's forbidden by you, might be the one thing meeting my specific needs. "

Discover yourself confronting these lines as each page opens a door into someone else's reality. As individual narratives play a fundamental role in a truism that could easily be your own.

* * *

EMBRACE is a collection of adult situations
penned in a poetic format

Amour

"......*Love give naught but itself
and takes naught but from itself.
Love possesses not nor
would be possessed.
For love is sufficient
unto love......*"

Kahlil Gibran

AMOUR

I read you like the petals
of the roses I bring
penning your essence in the
atrium of my recollections

I see your face in the rising sun
hear your voice afloat
a summer breeze
your tender kiss begets
a mystic charm
you are the nexus
of my existence

In your love my phoenix rises
to a festival of pinnacles
a life moved independent
of old poems and ancient writings
who shall I quote my love?

Whose words express the
burning passions that
elongate my days and
forestall my nights

Behold the radiance of your beauty

the quintessence of your loving

the impress of your body

abut mine

my love

my one and only love

MY BELOVÉD

Haste me to your bed
my belovéd
bathe me in the
lushness of your girth
surge my tempting vessel
quench my cravings
storm the waters
of my crashing waves

Harmonize the words
I leave unspoken
grant the silent wishes
that I make
love me as the moonbeams
love the ocean
swathe me in the warmth
of your embrace

Warm me in our afterglow
of loving
enfold me in the foyer
of your sway

kiss me long and hard
kiss me silent
chaff as evenings dusk
obscures our play

WET DREAMS

Your face is all I dream of all I see
your eyes, your lips, your mouth
how they entice me

Come near my love and pass within my gape
your staunch remains advance my lust
adorn my windswept shape

Pray bath me in the waters of your warmth
arid my passions with your tongue
pray lay me in your swarth.

Your lips inflame within my hidden place
our bodies rise within the storm
of kisses that you trace

Embrace me now before the waking hour
bed me once more within this dream
before my marrow sours

I love you as the rivers love the seas
engage my pool of thrashing waves
induce sweet bliss, I plea

19

Your face is all I dream of all I see
the dampened sheets and smells of musk
how they entice me.

FOREPLAY

You finger the zones that
satisfy and excite me
birthing caterpillars
into grandiose butterflies

With serene adept
you breeze
my cavernous oasis
embody the radiance
my secret places hide

Drenched within the beauty
of your coveting
your salacious dalliance
breeds my carnal
screams

You the sole begetter
of my savoring
preamble to the pinnacles
I'll reach

foreplay

21

YOUR KISS

Your gentle kiss
your tongue
touching mine

roaming and moving
about the inside of
my mouth

sweet and just a bit sticky
like the feel of warm honey
on an index finger
from a sunburned jar

on a passionately hot
summer day

your kiss

BEING

Nature moves through me
with unrivaled passion
embodying her radiance
skimmed in her vastness
beading ringlets of moisture
on sun drenched skin
bathed in desire
I touch her

Odious to self
exposed to my fervor
her balmy her sodden
engulfs my desires
roaming and sparring
my passions eroding
in waves of rushed ardor
I fondle

Squirting and spurting
in boiling contractions
purged in the gorging
sweet nectar exploding
vile in the rapture

of cyclical stroking
as fluids implode
our dawning

A soaked cement round
beading ringlets of moisture
a steaming hot ground
boiling remnants of pleasure
engulfed in her beauty
beguiled by her rhythm
Nature's hot summer days
besiege me

Adultére

*".....The course of true love
never did run smooth...."*

Shakespeare

INFIDELITY

Soft lips in avid foreplay
sinuously bathed in a viscid liquor
dotingly drained
from a frame now fraught
in a dark cold room
she suckles

austerely aroused she savors
oral pleasures beguiling
austere
relished now laden
once flaccid now firm
for her savoring swallows
I pay

on the edge of a sullied box-spring
in a corridor of old urine and mold
I bathe in the pinnacle
of her wandering tongue
of fellatio's rhythms and strokes

lost in an oral afterglow
bathed in a viscid liquor

27

drenched in the juices
of sewage and grime
old germs old grudge

old crimes

ADULTERY

Where were we meant to be
in the yesterdays of our lives?
is fate so fragile that time alone
has changed our course?

In love we came together,
open hearts and anxious minds.
in inert reprisal we grew apart,
open hearts and anxious minds.

Nostalgia now surrounds us
in this subtle place and time.
whilst waves of fury entrenched within
are eating our souls alive.

Does life offer no more than rampage
does fate protect the enraged heart
must our lives belong to someone else
are we void dignity, void pride?

Where were we meant to be
in the yesterdays of our lives

in love you blindly took my hand
I held your heart in mine.

BREACHED

Within these walls
our bed has lost its value
a chilling breeze
cuddles satin sheets
and a plush duvet

in the warmth
of these four walls
we gather in silence
your stoic glare
begetting the worst
foretelling your prey

for better or worse
grows mostly worse
in this deafening silence
antipathy from me
a callous resentment
befalls from you

afraid of leaving
loathing the notion of staying
in this deafening stillness

we duly avow

divorce
where art thou

CUCKOLD

Betwixt her thighs
encircling her nipples
within her venter
cascading her back

"désir sexuelle"
to be taken
a coveting passion
to be touched

jutting limp
a spouse surrenders
grown complacent
given up
a prostrate lorn
a sex drive dwindled
incompetent
a pride expunged

business weekends
lunchtime quickies
pristine lovers
and pioneered friends

wives and mothers
sisters daughters

"putain masculine"
a life abhorred

upscale rooms
and turnpike hideaways
for the rich
and the dirt wrenched poor
there she'll pay
to keep it private
laissez-faire
her male whore

Me faire l'amour

"just when I think I have escaped

it plagues my dreams

assaults my soul

hones in on my helplessness

knows my weakness

calls me from an ancient

beautiful lustful Eden place

naked souls - barren - unearthed

spinning fables of love - lust - longing

primordial scrolls of remembrance

it sees me - reassures me

just when I think I have escaped"

Excerpt from
"THE HAUNTING"
By TPS

NARCISSISTIC LOVER

Excuse me
may I break your rules
and touch you
I want to feel our fingers
intertwined
your taboos of confiding lust
are lucid
may I place your hands
between my sultry thighs

apologies for unnerving
whilst you're resting
this emptiness consumes
my every thought
will you touch me if I promise
not to bate you
I recognize the keen of
your disgust

forgive annoying flaunts
of warmth and passions
I wear them in the sadness
of my eyes

my wedding vows preclude

adulterous pleasures

these reins of marriage vest

my deafening cries

excuse me

may I break your rule

and stroke you

my stretched libido seeds

an odious thatch

my riotous passions crave

clitoral pleasures

at times a woman needs

a human touch

SOMETIMES I TOUCH MYSELF

In the feigning shadows
a solstice moon
reticent of perilous
ashen and wan
in nighttime pockets
soft wet skin

I fondle whereof
passion lingers
I finger where ardor
doth taste

in and out
in a myriad of groping
bathed in moonlight
on glistening sheets
limbs tighten
as fervor dawns entry
wetness souses
as pinnacles shriek

in syrupy wet dreams
blood rushes

earth shudders

as orgasms peak

on the rancid floor of

this penal stall

I fondle

I finger

I dream

RAW SEX

Womanhood overwhelms me
wetness rushing glands
waves of arousal boiling blood
inflame my yin
my yang

passion's breathing pinnacles
plateaus a hymen's tear
shades of rose bejewels my thighs
beguile my yin
my yang

a pubic arch ascending
a clitoris unconstrained
erectile tissues fill with blood
induce my yin
my yang

raw sex overwhelms me
locked in this infamous game
a vaginal fornix enraptures
enthralling my yin
my yang

your roving tongue provokes me

excites my clitoral head

waves of euphoria engage my yin

eruptions

still my yang

TO SAPPHO OF LESBOS

I love her

the curves of her body
the length of her legs
the smell of her breath
when she leans and
reads over my shoulder

albeit
she is married to a man
who is obtrusive

I am married to a demon
who leaves stains
yet
in my daytime dreams
I covet her

the camber of her buttock
the richness of her breast
the stealth of the panoramic
vastness between her thighs
her warm moist lips

kissing the back of my neck

"though she's not........
whilst I'm not...... "

yet
my passion ponders loudly

why not?

Amour brisé

"........ We can live without religion and meditation, but we cannot survive without human affection......"

The Dalai Lama

ARMED

Our loving is an accident
a cancer

I suffer from
the blacks and blues
bestowed

there is no charm
in our comings
or our goings

our way of loving
is a special effects
gone wrong

we dance the bloody dance
of two lives ending
of castaways on life's
intrepid shore

each time I close my eyes
I feel I'm falling
the gates of hell spread wide

its open doors

half-heartedly you loved
and once adored me
whole-heartedly I chased
a shooting star

know now
this is the last time
you'll accost me
your soul is his
your mortal body's
mine

THE RIFT

You allowed the silence to happen
to keep me unseen
unheard

you discarded the pieces of our
broken vows
separating my present
from your past

I've tried to fathom
your lewdness
why your phoenix
continuously burns

tried to strip your lies
from my bitterness
learn which sex is alluring
your charms

I met someone the other day
when he looked at me
I felt seen

when I removed my clothes
spread wide my legs
and beckoned

I was heard

REVERIE

I thought we'd like
the same music
read the same books
see the same movies

I was wrong

I thought short of merit
our lives would dance freely
in our own clumsy way
we'd see ourselves
in one another

I thought

I thought candle light and flowers
would swirl waves of passion
we'd like the same wine
confront the same
dogmas

thought you'd be love's metaphor
the imagery I fashioned

51

we'd be souls entwined in time
inseparable together

I was wrong

thought I'd never be bored
thought I'd never be lonely
thought your touch
would make me tremble
thought our love
would warm and cuddle

thought what's yours
would be mine
thought what's mine
would be ours

thought I'd free myself
to be myself
thought I'd see myself
in you

I was wrong

INCUBUS

Inhumanly spectacular a

metaphor of addiction

my being consumed

invites penetration

in plateaus of orgasms

blood lust running rapid

fangs bruising and piercing

it rapes me

Its piquant of kisses in

exciting new places

wittingly avoided

gregariously awaken

I should scream should escape

suppress murmurs of relish

I should shroud it with scratches

hide physical pleasures

it intoxicates it humbles

it rapes me

alluring blood from its lips

sexual bliss born of violence

compounded orgasms

rich in filth drawn in evil

deadly female genitalia

now his for the taking

darkness fades into daybreak

it rapes me

SEASONED

The gray softly rounded my face
highlighting the
wrinkles and imperfections
that comes with time

an old chipped mirror
reflects large sad eyes
darkened by a lifetime
of secrets

black and white lies
once shades of gray
blend sands of time
with lovelorn gold leaf

lost and alone
in a wasteland of oldness
passion befalls its rush
in vain

*"mirror mirror on the wall
who art thou"*

*My undying love revels in the
joviality of your happiness
warms you in your time of sadness
cuddles you as you face
life's challenges*

*like springtime vines
our lives entwined*

I miss you

THE FIDDLER

He exhumed carnal pleasures
from a piece of wood and
flawlessly placed strings
inflaming erogenous zones
awakening his libido

Stradivari

Deriving his pleasures
drawing his passion
teasing non-genital areas of arousal
with vibratos and harmonics
emotionally masturbating in
successions of arpeggios
ascending and descending
back and forth
in and out
in a rebirth of stimulation

Amati

Restricted and controlled
by the hairs of his bow

a chaste Baroque swells

drops of scented moisture blush

sharps flatten

flats steep in ecstatic fulfillment

clefs dangling on staffs

beguiled in his afterglow

Paganini

Tu me manques

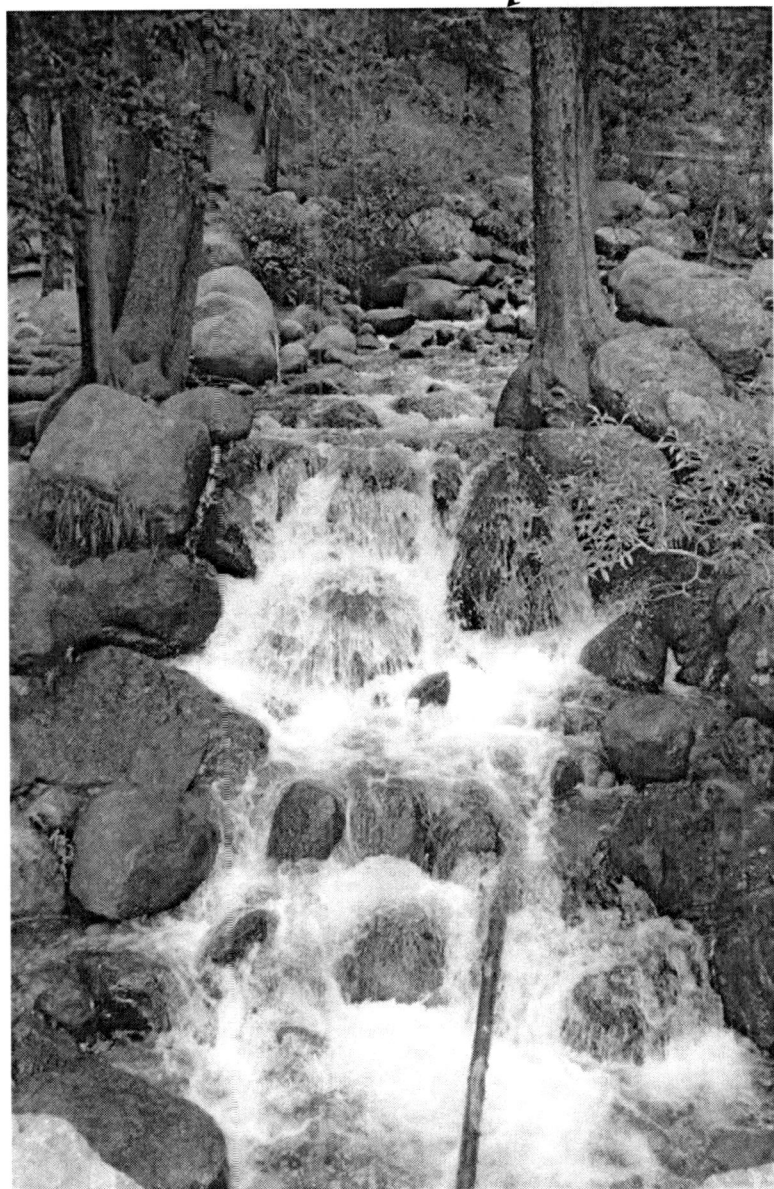

*".....Love is too young to know
what conscience is,
Yet who knows not conscience
is born of love?...."*

Shakespeare

I MISS IT

He slashed the passion from
my blossoms, the color
from my stems

in avoidance he uprooted
all that was good and
warm and kind

sunshine now rejects me
stars avoid my weeping eyes

petals lay agape
with longing, crazed with
lush desires

hatred strewn on
northern winds besiege
my very soul

fools rush in where
weeds absorb the riches
of my soils

tears cascade in drops
of rain, they taint, pollute
despoil

intimacy eludes me
and I miss it

HIS WAR

Attacked by an enemy
captured and tortured
released in a minefield
wounded contorted
rough sex his new ally
denial his nemesis

he listens

secured in a cell
for beating his wife
lost in a haze
of flashbacks and dreams
wishing for death
locked in his screams

he listens

loneliness melds with
salt ridden tears
cornered and squared
each stain a mistake

envisioning her face

reliving her screams

he listens

HER WAR

Left in a bridal suite
ardent and lonely
last minute orders
Afghanistan calling
a sweet kiss goodbye
a ride to the station

she listens

months devoid intimacy
craved copulation
weary of dildos
self-gratification
surrounded by prospects
lured by invitations

she listens

loneliness melds to
infidelity's clutch
exposed in the bedlam
of it was just sex
cornered and squared

reliving his fist
muffling her screams

she listens

Translations

Amour · Love

Adultére · Adultery

Me faire l´amour · Make love to me

Amour brisé · Broken Love

Tu me manques · I miss you

Désir sexuelle – Sexual Desire

Putain masculine – Male Prostitute

"......Ever has it been that love knows not its own depth until the hour of separation......"

Kahlil Gibran.

Content by Subject

*"....Genuine poetry can
communicate before
it is understood......"*

T.S. Eliot

ABOUT THE AUTHOR

Shirley Howard Hall is the author of *ONE DAY; Life, Love and Controversy in Middle America, LISTEN* and a contributor to *Candy* and *Stars in Our Hearts: Moments.* She is the recipient of various awards and her work has appeared in newspapers, magazines and blogs nation wide.

An advocate for peace, freedom, and equality she challenges social, economical, religious, and political agendas through controversial, provocative, insightful, and inspirational poetry and essays. As a voice for the people behind the story her poems minister to current affairs and emotions; befitting life's challenges - and our times.

As a speaker she has presented her poems in colleges and universities, in social and professional venues, and in 1980 by special invitation to Ambassador Terrance Todman at the American Embassy in Madrid Spain.

As owner of *More Than Words* her vitae ranges from specialized consignment pieces to corporate, group, and individual announcements, pamphlets, and personalized greetings.

A diversified writer, widely read poet, and noted public speaker, her controversial bodies of work have been used in university classes and is read and appreciated worldwide.

SHIRLEYHALLPOET.LLC
P O Box 3938
Broken Arrow, Oklahoma 74013

Email: www.shirleyhallpoet@yahoo.com
www.shirleyhallpoet.com
www.shirleyhallpoet.net
www.shirleyhallpoet.blogspot.com

Linked in   facebook

twitter

Other collections by: SHIRLEY HOWARD HALL

ONE DAY; Life, Love and Controversy in Middle America

Using the richest of language, ONE DAY highlights the complexities facing mankind today. Writing in first person the author opens avenues of understanding by becoming the voice of the people behind the story. From the chains of slavery to the horrors of abuse, from the terror of the battlefield, to the breakdown of the family, a whirlwind of emotions rise and fall as the author embodies an excruciating honesty in a most unexpected format. In this collection the author openly discusses, war, slavery, race, health care, crime, religion, spousal and child abuse, mental illness, suicide, and so much more. Through a wonderful provocative prose, she makes these voices heard.

Copyright 2007. Second edition published by Total Publishing and Media 2009; ISBN: 978-0-9798538-8-3

LISTEN

LISTEN takes a reader deep into the conscientious of the socially, economically, and culturally challenged of the world. Confronting the communal stigmas of not fitting in, it is a first person journey into the poignant lives of those who fail to flourish in today's society. In this collection of poems the author compels us to look at the mistreated and enslaved. Hopeless and helpless abused and disenfranchised. The author forces us to acknowledge and at times concede to the darkness that masks their faces.

Published by Total Publishing and Media 2009
ISBN: 0-88144-481-2

Praise for
Shirley Howard Hall's
Poetry

This is powerful and moving. I love and appreciate how you create such poignant art with your words. Not only are they beautifully written, they 'SAY' something that all need to hear - not with eyes & ears only but with their heart. They stir me to greater consciousness and I thank you for that....Joe

A Poet for Our Age,
By **Annette Sandberg** (Pittsburgh, PA) - **This review is from: One Day (Paperback)**
Shirley Hall's collection of poems cuts to the heart of our human condition, offering moments of sadness, madness and tenderness. Ms. Hall is definitely a poet to watch, and I highly recommend this book.

Beautifully written!,
By **Renee Kohl** **This review is from: One Day: Life, Love and Controversy in Middle America (Paperback)**
The book One Day is comprised of thirty-eight poems beautifully written by Shirley Howard Hall. Hall's poems individually or collectively are humanistic in nature--concerned with human welfare, values, and dignity. Her section entitled Life is my favorite. In these poems Hall reflects on how she viewed the world and her place in it during different stages of her life. After reading this section I found myself scrutinizing my feelings about life as a child versus later times. I feel those reading this book of poetry will be inspired by its content, and impressed by the poet's style. This book should be read by as many people as possible and would

be great for a reading circle because of its wealth of issues.

The next Maya,
By **Delores J. Jordan** (Mobile, Alabama) **This review is from: One Day (Paperback)**
Shirley's work is beautiful poetry combined with social statements. She tackles some very taboo subjects and writes such excellent poetry you don't realize she's pulled you into a very hot topic. These poems make you think as well as have you enjoy fine poetry and beautiful words. I highly recommend this book.

Shirley
I just got done reading your book. And I must say that it took me off guard. In a good way. I like how you divided your poetic subjects. Very good. I have a small library and your book will make a fine addition. Something to read again in the future, like other choice books of mine. Your first poem is a great introduction for the book. I also was very impressed by your poem about Dr. King. I wrote a poem about him over a year ago. I will publish it in the future. He was a great man and a greater mind. Thank you for the support and keep me informed about any more publications of yours.

J.W. Bowers

Shirley
I just wanted you to know that I bought a copy of your book and it arrived yesterday. I have read it...and it is amazing! It is everything I thought it would be Thank you for sharing of yourself and your passions.

Naome

Shirley, I don't know why others haven't said this yet, but sister this poem KICKS ASS to the 10th degree! I'm putting you on my wall of fame. I Should have done that a while back. I apologize! Your heart and soul just over flows with thought provoking words in such a way that it makes the reader take a hard look at themselves and the world around them.

Much Respect,
Keeb
Posted by Keeb Knight

Shirley - How beautifuly said. I say thank YOU for being so kind as to share your unique way of weaving words into beautiful tapestries for all of us to enjoy. I cannot tell you how many times your poems have touched my life and sometimes given me the strength to keep going I might otherwise not have had. You give a voice to those who cannot be heard, you give to those who might otherwise not be mourned. Thank you from the bottom of my heart for being you. For the encouragement you have given me to keep writing.

Happy New Year.
Your friend,
Maggie....Indiana

"Dear Libra woman I loved your poems. Insightful, heart-rending, ripe and sage. Wisdom is thy name. Sharing your self is a path to ones' heart and soul."
Lara....March 2009

"Shirley, your writing transcends boundaries, brings us to new realizations and understandings. Thank you for

the many critically vital issues you address and the sheer beauty of your words, the depth of your compassion and the transparency of your message. You are a truly remarkable talent on the writing stage. I embrace your courage and faith in mankind."
DON
BC Canada,

"Shirley,. I cried as I read this. For me, it's the portrait of struggle between life and death-between good & evil ......the cost & the prize of living. I especially appreciate how you balance the message of any cause for which you write, passionately illustrating pain and injustice, yet pursuing answers for improvement without bitter hatred and doom. I have not yet felt any sense of victimization or hopeless despair in your writings - but always a pull to seek out a better and more loving way to make a difference in the world around me. Be blessed always"
xoxo
Debra...Tennessee

"True to form..... Shirley! You never cease to amaze me with your talent for addressing important social and life issues! Simply fantastic and well written "
J.Beck
Ireland

"Sweet Shirley, Another amazing insight to the complexities of the mind... So many times I am embraced when you show me another's world... Thank you my dear friend for sharing... Forever and a day,"
LoriLane
Las Vegas

"I need to read intelligent works to take my mind from my loneliness, pain and lost feelings...and finding you, has been a gift far beyond what I have expected... I come to your page to view all you display and I find comfort and peace...thank you.....
sincerely,".... Ami
Pennsylvania

"Shirley, you have outdone yourself!!!
Thank you for sharing your brilliance, my friend.
xoxo,"
Julie~
London, England

"Shirley, this was moving. SERIOUSLY POIGNANT.
bold. unapologetic. REAL.
I was gripped the whole way through.
I think you're a marvelous poet. Thank you for allowing me into your world."
S.Smith
Oklahoma

"I especially thank you for your sensitivity and keen insight. Your work radiates a wonderful, unsympathetic humanity that is not merely words, but also action most needed."
Kevin
Centrallia, Pennsylvania

"This particular style of writing carries me away and I become so drawn into it...very inviting! I marvel at your skill to sweep me away in your words.
Thank you for this."
Julie
Australia

Shirley -
"Congrats!
What a great creative outlet.
I particularly liked BETWEEN THE LINES.
I'm proud to call you my friend."
 - Mike

CPSIA information can be obtained at www.ICGtesting.com
Printed in the USA
LVOW061952030612

284488LV00002B/145/P